SLEEPING WITH NEIGHBORS

From the Debauched Squad Goals Erotica Series

M.C. Byrd

Be sure to go to the site and subscribe to the newsletter. You do not want to miss out on new books or chances to win prizes.

Kindle readers be sure to follow M.C. Byrd on Amazon to be notified of new releases as they become available.

CONTENTS

INTRODUCTION

Malcolm was running late for his biweekly brunch with his friends because he was entangled with twins from the night before. There was still the matter of dealing with their sister as well. Malcolm's friends will not believe what happened to him--that it is probably not true. They might not even be surprised. Check out Malcolm meeting his neighbors and tune in for the rest of the Debauched Squad Goals Erotica Series.

BRUNCH

Malcolm was running late for his biweekly brunch with his friends. It was a late night for him. Typically a late afternoon brunch, for some, this may seem like enough time to recover from a night of fun, but how was he going to leave this bed with these people without it being awkward.

Malcolm sat up and realized there was no sneaking out of this apartment. One of the home's occupants was already up and moving in the kitchen. There was a twin on both sides of him, but they were definitely sleeping soundly. Who was Malcolm going to climb over or wake up?

*   *   *

Malcolm walked up to the table that his four friends were sitting at. Grace, the spunkiest of the bunch said, "How do we pick the place closest to you and you *still* manage to be late?" Malcolm smiled and picked up a piece of fried plantain with his hand as he flopped down into the booth.

"Well peasants, a king can never be late," Justin says in a dry voice "and what makes you a king, Malcolm?"

"Well, the way I was serviced last night, of course."

Jacob laughed. "I imagine that this story will only add to your Hoe Resume, not make you a king." Grace grimaced and chimed in, "Now Jacob, some of us just enjoy sex. We do not think of it as a chore or a reward for good behavior."

Jacob replied, "You talk to me like I am a prude." Grace replied, "No, we talk to you like you have missionary sex in the dark, and your version of spicing it up is doing it doggy style." The table chuckled, including Jacob.

Tracie chimed in "No, we talk to you like you are always trying to convert an obvious hoe into a housewife." Jacob scoffed and retorted, "Weren't we just talking about people not being hoes and having sex for joy?"

Fred said, "Yes, but you keep attracting women with no skills, who obviously want to use you to become a housewife." Jacob retorted "What is wrong with being a housewife? My mom was one, and I would prefer if my wife stayed home."

Tracie answered, "Nothing-- if that is what you and your spouse decide, but the people you keep bringing around are mean spirited, plotting vultures. You know, the type that will murder you one day after the life insurance policy fully kicks in." Fred added, "Sitting there enjoying your morning coffee, and you end up keeling over."

"You all are so dramatic," said Jacob. "No, this story I am about to tell about this past week is about to be dramatic," replied Malcolm.

"You all will not believe how I managed to get a family in bed." Fred chuckled, "This sounds like the section of a porn site that only people in Kentucky or somewhere in the south lookup."

Grace added an antidote, "They use to make couples in Oklahoma get a blood test before they got married." The table erupted in laughter, but it seemed like no one was surprised.

Malcolm said in an excited tone, "I took it a bit further than perusing the section." Jacob said, "I don't want to know, but I want to know."

MEETING SOMEONE NEW

Malcolm was pinged on his phone in a dating app.

NotAllN: Hey Wi11Penitr8, you are looking really hot. I like playing drunk Mario Kart and playing pickup games of basketball too.

Malcolm scrolled through the guys' photos and determined that NotAllN deserved a response.

Wi11Penitr8: Hi NotAllN, you are pretty hot yourself. I love your dogs, it is a super cute pug and that great dane has a gorgeous grey coat.

NotAllN: Yea, I love Chuck and Flash. Unfortunately Flash lives with my parents, our apartment is not large enough, and he needs space to roam free.

Wi11Penitr8: Oh, are you home now?

NotAllN: Yea, why?

Wi11Penitr8: I just noticed that we are super close in proximity, and I was wondering if you actually lived here or were visiting a friend or something.

NotAllN: Is that the only reason you asked? ;-)

Wi11Penitr8: Kind of yes. You living here makes me feel a bit better. This is not exactly a crappy apartment, and I at least know that a background check has been run on you.

NotAllN: Now that we know that each of us at least passes a background, why don't you invite me over?

Wi11Penitr8: You aren't going to offer to buy a guy a drink first? O:-D

NotAllN: I can bring over some wine and order a pizza?

Wi11Penitr8: Why not just invite me to your place?

NotAllN: I live with my twin and younger sister, one of them is home now.

Wi11Penitr8: Come over to 303.

Malcolm gets a knock on his door. NotAllN has a bottle in his hand. He is gorgeous. He is a little taller than Malcolm, so he must be about six-three.

He has twinkling green eyes and curly brown hair. He has freckles dusting his cheeks and a well-cared for beard. He has on black sweatpants and a muscle blue shirt on-- showing off his muscled abs. You can see all the veins popping in his shredded arms.

The guy stretches out his hand and says, "Hi, I am Allen".

"Hey, I am Malcolm." Malcolm steps back and lets him in.

"I get it. Not all in also sounds like Allen." Allen chuckled, "Yeah but it is mostly for sexual innuendo versus a play on my name." Malcolm, looked down at Allen's crotch for a bit and said, "I might actually believe you." They headed over to the couch and Allen put the bottle down.

"I wasn't thinking. Let me grab glasses and a bottle opener. You can pick anything you want. Netflix is already queued up." Malcolm came back into the living room with glasses and a meat and cheese tray.

Allen said, "You just have meat and cheese trays?" Malcolm replied, "Actually yeah, I don't really eat the crackers, and all the meat and cheese is a high source of fat and protein. It is a cheap snack that keeps me in my macro goals."

Allen replied, "I see. Are you trying to get bigger, show more definition?"

"Mostly to maintain my current physique."

"Well, it is a nice one."

"That is nice of you. You are pretty jacked."

"Yea. I am a personal trainer, and I do a bit of social media influencing for athletic wear."

"That is cool. I am actually a social media manager. My portfolio is kind of eclectic. Banks, boutiques, sporting goods, and other random stuff. But did you pick a show or a movie?"

Allen was sitting when Malcolm came back in with the glasses.

"Yea, a cheesy rom-com if you do not mind."

"I do not mind at all."

Malcolm poured them glasses of wine after he uncorks the chilled, white wine and put the bottle back on the table.

Allen sat to the far left of the couch, holding his wine in one hand, with his arm outstretched on the couch. Malcolm takes this as an invitation and sits right next to Allen, placing his head on Allen's sexy chest and swinging his legs up on the couch.

Allen draped his arm on Malcolm's shoulders, and they just watched the movie for a while. When Allen finished his drink, he placed the glass on the table next to the couch. Malcolm wordlessly passed him his glass so that he could do the same.

Allen began to rub Malcolm's nipple through his shirt, then he pinched it a bit. Malcolm's breath got caught in his chest for a little bit. He likes a bit of pain and some surprise. Malcolm said, "You might as well begin to do what you really want."

Allen took that as permission and a challenge. He got up from the couch and got in front of Malcolm on the couch. Malcolm proceeded to swing his legs down to put his feet on the floor and left his knees spread out the width of Allen's very broad shoulders.

Allen proceeded to unbutton Malcolm's pants and pull his penis through the open boxer hole. Malcolm tilted his hips up and decided to push his lounge pants down his ass, along with his boxers. He left them at mid-thigh. Allen went ahead and pulled his pants down and off his legs.

Allen ran his hands up Malcolm's thighs and did not hesitate to push his head down onto Malcolm's very thick erection. Allen began to deep throat and swallow down on Malcolm's dick with intense intentions.

Malcolm ran his hands across the couch multiple times before he put his hand in Allen's curly hair and put the other on his shoulder and started to do little thrusts up. He could not seem to sit still during this amazing blowjob.

The light hair pulling and thrusting seemed to activate even more enthusiasm from Allen. He sucked on the head of Malcolm's penis then swallowed his balls and grasped the shaft. He did this wicked turning and up and down motion. Malcolm made an audible noise where he sucks in a lot of air and says, "Fuck, you are really good at that!"

Allen stopped sucking on Malcolm's balls and began to suck on his dick again. This time, licking and sucking with another kind of furiosity while he is turning his head and rubbing on Malcolm's balls.

This went on for a bit and at this point, Malcolm had almost scooted his butt completely off the sofa. Allen sucked on Malcolm's balls, then licked behind them until Malcolm shouted, "Yessssss, right the fuck there!" Allen began to lick lower and even suck on the spot.

Allen put a finger in his mouth, while he is sucking dick, then he proceeded to put his finger on Malcolm's anus. He pressed gently but firmly. While still sucking his dick and rubbing his balls, Malcolm relaxed and tried to stop clenching his ass because Allen is fairly insistent.

Malcolm, really enjoying this, says, "If you don't stop, you will get a load in your throat". Allen does not relent and after another minute, Malcolm released his load with an audible roar and Allen swallowed.

He kind of pushes Allen off when he does not stop after a moment. He pulled Allen up and kissed him for a bit. Malcolm said, "Give me a sec to return the favor."
Allen frowned a little, "I will actually need to take a rain check, I have to get to the gym. I have a client. I really was not planning on whipping your penis out on this first date." Malcolm laughed, "Who the fuck needs intentions when the best things are always surprises." They kissed for a little longer, then Allen left.

THEN SOMEONE ELSE

Malcolm kept watching the movie and eating on his couch. Still feeling kind of drained from the amazing blow job he received. He received another message from the same site.

Zo4You: Hey Wi11Penitr8, you look hella good in that boxer short shot. You a model or something?

Malcolm flipped through this guy's profile and is a little taken aback. Is Allen messing with him? This guy looked just like Allen, but they have very different profiles and interests. Are Allen and Zoe4You messing with him together?

He goes back to Allen's profile; it shows that he is over a mile away. While this Zo4You is zero miles away. Allen did mention living with a brother, but did he say twin or just brother? Malcolm thought about this but shrugged and thought, *you only live once.*

Wi11Penitr8: Hey man, no I am not a model, but thanks for the stroke of the ego.

Zo4You: Are you looking to get something stroked?

Wi11Penitr8: That was super straightforward, LOL

Zo4You: You kind of set it up for me by not saying ego boost and your screen name is Will Penetrate; I figured I would shoot my shot.

Wi11Penitr8: That is pretty reasonable. What did you have in mind?

Zo4You: Well, it looks like you are pretty close. Come over to my place. I am in 220.

Wi11Penitr8: Ok, I will be over shortly.

Zo4You: No need in getting all done up for me; I already know you are hot.

Malcolm chuckles and thinks about how he is more so trying to wash away the scent of this guys brother and his release from himself. After a birdbath in his bathroom, Malcolm goes to Zo4You's place and knocks on the door.

When he walks in the apartment, it smells like watermelon and lemon. The guy hugs him in the doorway.

"So nice to meet you. I am Brandon."
"Hi, I'm Malcolm."

The guys must be twins; they look just alike. Malcolm says, "Wow, your place is really big. Mine is a lot smaller."
"That is probably because this is a three bedroom. I share it with my twin and our younger sister."

"Oh, how much younger?" "Barely eleven months, our parents were way too eager, clearly." "That is a lot of screaming toddlers."

By now, they have entered the kitchen.

"Take a seat man. Want a bottle of water?" "Sure," Malcolm says as he gets comfortable on the couch. Brandon begins walking over to the couch, and a woman is rushing from one of the rooms at the end of the hallway.

Malcolm turns his head and only gets a glimpse of her round apple shaped butt in a tight pencil skirt and blazer. Her hair is blowing in long, wavy curls behind her. He can see in her profile that she is wearing a dull pink lipstick.

She pays him little to no attention as she keeps moving out of the apartment door. Brandon sits down on the couch right next to him and hands him the water.

"Sorry about that. I really thought Augusta was already gone, she is really late going to meet her client."
"Oh, what does she do?" "Sells real estate."

Malcolm chuckles a little, "And what do you do?"
"I am a tattoo artist. Apprentice actually. I was in school for architecture, but I got kind of bored with it. After I got my first tat, I decided that I wanted to try it out and made the change almost a year ago."

"How did your family take it?"
"Well, they don't really influence what I do. It's my life. But I guess I was pretty lucky; they were not weird about it. I guess I am the bullheaded twin. Whatever I want to do; I just make it work."
"What was your first tat?"

Brandon stands up, pulls his lime green t-shirt off and shows off a crazy number of tattoos and a pierced nipple. He pulls the waistband down on his gym shorts and shows Malcolm a bird's nest with two birds that hatched and another one that was cracking through its shell.

Malcolm reached up and traced it with his finger, partially because the design was really interesting. The shading showed the touch of a real professional. The other reason was that he just wanted to touch him.

"Wow, this just looks like an interesting story." "Yea, at the time, I was really unsure. But already two years into architecture. I knew I did not want to do it, but I could not figure out what else I wanted to do. It seemed like my siblings had it all figured out. It is also the plague of the middle child."

"That's really heavy." "So is something else," Malcolm chuckled and said as he looked Brandon up and down, devouring his heavily muscled body and tattoo work. "What are we going to do about that?"

Brandon extended his hand, Malcolm allowed him to pull him up. They began kissing immediately; instant tongue thrashing. Brandon sucked on Malcolm's bottom lip and grabbed his ass.

Brandon broke off the kiss after a few minutes and led Malcolm to his room. It was fairly sparse. Malcolm could not tell if he had just moved in or if he just lived clutter free. There were a few large sketches of birds and dragons pinned to the wall; all in charcoal or black chalk.

Brandon wasted little time stripping Malcolm of his clothes and shucking his own shorts down. They resume kissing and Brandon used one hand to hold Malcolm by the waist, resting his fingertips on the swell of his butt. Brandon also had his other hand on Malcolm's balls.

He alternated massaging Malcolm's balls and stroking his dick. Brandon eventually says, "Let's wet this up a bit." He quickly spits on Malcolm's dick, bends over and deep throats his penis while still massaging his balls.

Malcolm groaned and thought about how lucky it was that he was getting two incredible blow jobs in one day. He finds himself thrusting a bit into Brandon's throat.

When Brandon stands straight up, Malcolm turns him around and pushes him onto the bed. Brandon settled himself onto his hands and knees. Malcolm spotted the condoms and lubricant on the bedside table when they came in, "Thank you for being all ready for me".

Malcolm spanked him again, hitting the fleshy part of his right, then his left butt cheek and then caught some of his right thigh.

Brandon seemed to push his ass up even higher and chanted a couple of, "Yesses".

Malcolm reached over and grabbed the lubricant, putting it on two fingers, rubbing it against Brandon's anus and gently pushing his finger in. He used his other hand to stroke Brandon's shaft and roll his balls in Malcolm's hand.

Brandon steadily pushed back a little as Malcolm thrusted in and out of his ass with his finger. Soon Malcolm inserted two fingers into Brandon's ass, but he does not try to insert them too far or stroke Brandon's insides.

Brandon and Malcolm were rock hard and eager at this point. Brandon said, "Fuck, put it in! That feels so good." Malcolm pulled his fingers out of Brandon, stepped back a little and bit Brandon's ass cheek.

He reached over and put a condom on. He spanked Brandon a couple more times and put the head of his penis into Brandon's ass. Brandon clenched, Malcolm hit him on the ass again.

"Don't fight it, take this dick Zo".

Brandon pushed his butt up a little; Malcolm put one hand on his waist and rubbed his back a little. Malcolm began to make shallow thrusts in and out of Brandon.

"You want some more don't you B?" Brandon did not answer, just panted and pushed back. Malcolm hit him on the ass again, "Answer me if you want some more."

"Yes, yes please, fuck me. I want some more." Malcolm pushed in further--still not too fast or too far, he knew he was a lot. Even for a very experienced bottom.

Once Malcolm got a steady and deep rhythm going, he reached around the front of Brandon and began to stroke his penis. Brandon began to moan even louder and more frequently. Malcolm popped him again on the butt. Then Brandon came all over his bedspread.

Malcolm let go of Brandon's penis as he started to cum and then started thrusting into him a little harder and faster. After a few more pumps, Malcolm was ready to cum. He pulled out of Brandon, pulled the condom off and spilled his cum on Brandon's butt.

Malcolm was kind of surprised he had so much cum left, especially after earlier with Brandon's brother Allen. Malcolm looked around but did not see any tissue or a wastebasket. He said, "Going to clean up a bit". He strolled out of the bedroom and looked for the bathroom.

All the doors were closed, and the first one that he opened was obviously Allen's room. He had boxes stacked in two of the corners, and there was a laundry basket with clothes spilling out of it. Along with an unmade king bed, Brandon only had a queen bed.

He closed the door and shuffled to the next door. He went into the bathroom, not bothering to close the door. The bathroom was not really decorated. There were also only two toothbrushes; the sister must have her own bathroom.

There were not any feminine products around. He pulled the condom off and dropped it into the trash. He peed and then washed his hands. Malcolm walked back to Brandon's room.

The bedspread was pulled off. Brandon either had a large blanket already on the bed, or he put one on it while Malcolm was away. He also had on shorts and was sitting on the bed against the headboard.

Malcolm's clothes were laid neatly on the bedside table. Brandon said, "I am a bit of a neat freak." Malcolm replied, "I am not messy or dirty, but I probably would not have stripped the bed or moved clothes in any order with a sense of urgency."

They chuckled and Malcolm moved out of the doorway over to his clothes. They talked as he got dressed. Malcolm was not invited to stay, and he had no interest to stay and run into Allen, so he left, and they hugged goodbye.

BACK TO BRUNCH

The table chuckled after Malcolm told this story. Jacob said, "I hear you but that does not make you a king." Grace agreed, "Yea, that was cool, but I actually do not expect any different from you. Fred and Tracie nodded in agreement.

Malcolm took a sip of his mimosa and laughed, "That was just the beginning of the story guys. That was ice tea without sugar. You all interrupted too quickly. What is left of the tea is scalding hot with sugar and berry flavors."

Fred replied, "Oh shit." As if it were choreographed, the group took another sip of their mimosas.

SOMEONE DIFFERENT

Malcolm was getting ready for bed. He was watching the Office to help zone himself out then he got an alert from a different dating site. He got a like from someone named Augusta.

She liked his hiking photo and her like was followed by a reply that said, "Hey, is this pic on the Eiger on your way to the Matterhorn? If yes, I have a super similar one in my profile."

Malcolm clicked Augusta's name and went through her profile. They took a very similar selfie-- potentially in the same spot. It was probably only different because he was so much taller.

Malcolm was a little over six feet while Augusta's profile said she was five six. She was a beautiful woman and seemed to pull off every style from business professional, athletic to sexy temptress in club wear.

She also seemed to switch up her hair color quite a bit. Augusta had a really hot photo of her and some of her friends. Their backs were to the camera, and they were all looking behind them at the photographer.

She had a fantastic ass. Malcolm messaged her and said, "You are absolutely correct, and it was such a fun hike." Malcolm actually did not enjoy that hike; he was hungover from the night before and could not convince his friends to do anything else.

He keeps the photo because outdoorsy guys or girls love it. It makes it seem like he is adventurous and also cares about his health. Augusta remarked, "It totally was. I love to get out of the city sometimes and breathe in some fresh air."

Malcolm loved air conditioning and hated bugs but he replied, "Totally! Nothing like being outdoors or pushing your body." Augusta then replied, "Are you free tomorrow? There is an open mic in Liberty that I want to check out."

Malcolm knew what she was talking about. "Howling Cart? The one every other Thursday?" Augusta replied, "Yes! I am assuming you have been before."

Malcolm was dating someone for a few months that dragged him there. Thankfully that guy has already left the city. "Yup, I have been there. I look forward to seeing you then.

The next night they met at Howling Cart. Some singers were great; a couple sucked. The spoken word also had the same range. One girl had a recently broken heart and hopped on stage trying to mend herself of a broken heart.

> Letter to a fuck boy
> I thought about wishing you well
> I thought about cursing you to hell
> I considered a few crimes
> But I knew you were not worth the time
> Would a pipe to the face
> Make this feeling of pain less than a disgrace
> Would some sugar in your gas tank
> Be considered by the law a little prank
> Letter to a fuck boy
> Who I thought I wanted to destroy
> Would showing up at where you work
> Be the right move to remove that smirk
> The one you gave me when you told me that other girl

meant nothing
And that I was truly something
Something special to you
But I know I ain't special boo
Well at least not to you
Letter to a fuck boy
Fuck you

Augusta and Malcolm kind of looked at each other after that performance. Augusta chuckled dryly, "I am willing to bet that in four weeks she has another poem about forgiveness and the importance of giving people a chance."

Malcolm laughed hard and said sarcastically, "I see you are an optimist and wishing them the best." Augusta smiled and said, "Of course. Only good things happen to people who are in love." Malcolm asked, "Are you looking for love?"

Augusta snorted, "I am looking for a good time. I think you do not have to look for love. When something is meant for you, it comes to you. You do not have to chase it; you do not have to convince it."

"That is essentially the opposite of every romance book and romantic comedy ever." "Maybe, but I like for my intentions to remain pure. I do not want to convince someone of my worth. I want them to see my potential, and I want to see theirs. Everyone else is a temporary good time; hopefully, they will not have a bunch of side effects."

Malcolm responded, "I surprisingly agree with that. It is kind of odd-- the number of people who enter a first date with the intent that you will be their person; their potential everything and then the other people who are wondering how fast they can get you out of your pants. No matter the gender."

Augusta tilted her head, "Elaborate on *no matter the gender*." Malcolm felt a little precarious now; he never knew how women would respond to him being bisexual. Often he found that they would tell him that he was just gay or that it was simply something that they were not into.

Even with gay men, many were not fazed by it, but some also questioned his sexuality. Whatever Augusta might think, Malcolm was going to be honest.

"Yes, that was not an overgeneralization on my part. I like males and females. I care more about who the person is. I have just noticed while dating that people want different things, and they do not communicate those expectations. For me, I have not had this moment where I connect with someone, and I need to keep them, and I want them to keep me."

He continued, "It has mostly just been fun or interesting enough for us to date exclusively. But I have been in situations with both genders where they get upset with me because we do not want the same thing."

"Look at you, just breaking hearts and disappointing people on both sides of the spectrum," Augusta said with a smirk on her face and a feeling of mirth in her expression. "Nice to know that it does not bother you."

Malcolm did not know that he was really fishing for confirmation.

"Yea, it really has no impact on what we are doing here," said Augusta in a calm tone.

"Is that because you have already decided that we have no future or something?" Malcolm did not know why he said that. He was not trying to persuade her into pursuing something, but something about her flippancy made him ask.

"Malcolm, I am not trying to be mysterious or trick you with my words, I meant it literally when I said that I am looking for a good time and willing to deal with all that comes with that--well that safely comes with that.”

Augusta chuckled again and that seemed to bring a lighter feeling back to their evening. The person singing on stage was singing a soft ballad in another language, so it was fairly easy to only focus on their conversation.

A duo got up to do some comedy, but their jokes were falling fairly flat. Malcolm said to Augusta, “Are you ready to get out of here?” Augusta nodded and stood up. Malcolm held the door for her, she thanked him and walked outside.

“Where do you want to head to?” asked Malcolm. Augusta said, “Toward Reynolds would be great. We can walk and talk.” Malcolm said, “Works for me. It's in the direction of home.”

Augusta said, “Oh cool. I love running around Reynolds Park.” “That’s neat. I live right next to it.”

Augusta asked, “Really, which one? I sell condos and houses in the area. I am pretty familiar with the apartments around too.”

“In Old Colony.” “SHUT UP! I live there too with my twin brothers.”

Malcolm could not believe it. This had to be Brandon and Allen’s sister. When he thought about it, they all totally looked alike. “You live with two guys, sounds like a messy situation.”

Augusta laughed, “It is not bad at all actually. I have my own bathroom, and Brandon is a real neat freak. He nags Allen, so he is okay about cleaning up around the apartment and keeping his mess in his room.”

“Why did you all decide to live together in an apartment instead of staying at home with your parents? I guess I am over assuming that you could stay with your parents.”

"That was a very fair question. Our parents adore us. We could have stayed home. With the three of us all working, there was no point in paying something expensive. We really just did not want to stay home, so we could have sex freely. It felt kind of disrespectful to parade guys in and out of our parents' house. The twins are basically sluts."

"What is it like for you if your brothers are parading girls in and out?" she barked out laughter. "That is kind of judgmental, isn't it? To assume they like girls. One brother is gay, the other is bi but tends to only really date guys lately."

This was not news to Malcolm seeing as he already slept with the twins, but he did wonder which one was bi. Malcolm was also surprised that he nor Augusta really got a good look at one another yesterday in her apartment.

Augusta asked Malcolm, "Have you considered a polyamorous relationship too?" Malcolm snorted, "Hardly. I do not think I could be into that. I am not opposed, but I am definitely not looking and nothing about it really sparks my interest. You?"

"Not me either. I do have two sets of friends trying it. One group is two girls and a guy. The other is two guys and a girl. I think, for me, I already suck at communicating. I would likely feel swallowed whole in something like that. Like you said, it has never really interested me. I cannot even think of a time when I crushed on two guys at once."

"What about a threesome or orgy though, have you had one?" "Yea, I have been a part of a couple, but those were just fun and functional. Nothing emotional in any of those situations." She paused, considering her next words.

"I was also the person brought in. It was not like it was my boyfriend and, we brought in a girl or a guy. It was nice to have a rumble of fun, then to be able to grab my things and leave. Not having to deal with the emotional part of that relationship."

"Augusta, you seem to be extremely self-aware but also like a part of you does not want to deal with your feelings." Augusta hummed and made a thoughtful noise like she was really mulling over what she wanted to say next.

"I am very introspective in some regards, but I often make a conscious effort to move my thoughts along. Sometimes sex and dating really is just fun for me. Sometimes I really like someone and want to make something work with them. Life and those experiences are great when I and those people have the same intentions. When we do not, shit kind of just falls apart."

Malcolm made a clicking noise with his mouth. He felt like her response made a lot of sense, but he also thought her logic was not very clear.

"Malcolm, you are thinking too hard about this. I simply try to figure out what is worth being hung up over or worth being up late night about, and I simply think that everything that is happening in my life or around me is worth that effort."

"Yea, but how do you actually decide that?" Augusta looked up at him a couple of moments before she answered, "There is not really this logical answer. It is more of a feeling. Most people make commitment decisions based on a feeling, not logic."

Malcolm thought about it for a moment and said, "I agree with that. I think I have dated people who hit all the checkboxes, but our chemistry did not sizzle. So it eventually faded."

They walked in silence for a block or two. Augusta hip checked him, well, she hit his thigh with her hip. Malcolm chuckled and put his arm around her.

"What are you thinking, Augusta?"

"If we should go to your place or mine." Malcolm thought about running into her brothers, "We can go to mine, don't want to disturb your bros."

Augusta chuckled, "That is half the fun. It is also kind of fun to remind them that they are not the only ones in the house. Plus I want to show you something."
"Are you sure about that?" asked Malcolm. He was really trying to figure out a way to go back to his apartment without raising any alarm with her.

"Yea, I am sure. Do not worry; my brothers are not home. We can protect your modesty", she said laughing and bumping him with her hip again. The next block was their apartment.

Malcolm found himself leading her back to her apartment and had to remind himself to fall back behind her. When they walked into her place, she placed her clutch on the counter, turned around and hopped up. She wrapped her legs around Malcolm, and he caught her while keeping his balance.

His hands immediately clutching Augusta's butt. She writhed against his hardening dick and took over their kiss by thrusting her tongue in and out of his mouth. He liked how feisty she was and willing to take charge.

Augusta pulled away from Malcolm's face, "Take us to my room." Malcolm was mindful enough to say, "Which way?" She began to kiss the side of his face, lick his ear, and nibble and suck on his neck.

"Left, and left again to the end." She resumed licking and sucking on his neck, and she began to rub and pinch on his nipple. When they were fully into her room, she hopped down and began to take his clothes off.

"What about you?" he said. "You will see me. Do not worry, but I want to see that huge dick that was rubbing against me" When she had him naked with his pants and underwear hanging around his feet, she pulled off her shirt and slipped to her knees.

Augusta put one hand on his thigh, took the other and cupped his balls. She said, "What a big pretty dick you have." Malcolm was about to respond, but she quickly put his balls in her mouth and was doing this intense thing where she was sucking on them while tonguing them.

Malcolm yelped a quick, "Oh shit that is fantastic." Then she popped them out and began to suck on the head of his penis.

Her mouth was incredibly wet. She pulled his penis out her mouth and spit on it while still holding onto his balls. She sucked on his dick some more then went back to sucking on his balls. She took his penis and then began to slap herself with his penis.

Malcolm could not believe his luck. He wondered where the hell these siblings learned to suck dick from. Augusta pulled away and stood up gracefully. Malcolm felt captivated by her. She took off her clothes, he moved to help her with her front clasping bra. He unhooked it but did not take it off.

He bent forward and sucked on her breast. He alternated between each, going from touching and clutching around her entire breast to pinching and flicking each nipple. She seemed to tire of this though.

She tapped his shoulder and said, "Malcolm, lay on the bed, part your legs slightly." He obeyed her wishes. She slipped on top of him but in a sixty-nine position. She put her bald pussy in his face, and she began to suck his dick again, being fairly clear about what she expected from him.

Malcolm put both of his hands on her butt and seemed to part her cheeks and dove his tongue into her pussy. He licked at her seem, from her clit to her anus. He sucked on her clit, hard and then soft.

Alternating hard and soft licks, he eventually started moving his face in a clockwise motion on her vagina. Augusta loved it and started grinding on his face a bit with her enthusiasm.

Augusta stopped sucking Malcolm's dick with a large pop. She turned around and rested along his waistline, seemingly thrusting her breast in his face again. Malcolm grabbed both of her breasts and played with them. She chuckled and licked around his lips.

"I like licking my pussy from around your mouth." She reached over him and into a drawer in her nightstand. Augusta pulled a condom out and then wiggled from Malcolm's grasp. She leaned back on her hind parts while Malcolm sat up on his elbows. She rolled the condom down on him, tossing the condom wrapper onto the floor.

Augusta smiled, "Ready for the ride of your life?" Malcolm chuckled, leaned forward more, and hit Augusta on the butt with both of his hands and then leaned all the way back. He said, "Absolutely".

She got up on her toes and positioned his dick at her entrance while using her other hand on his thigh to keep her balance. She then began to go up and down on Malcolm's dick, occasionally grinding her hips in clockwise and counterclockwise motions. He could not believe his good fortune. Her pussy was so tight and wet.

She then went down to her knees while straddling him. He thought that she was about to call it quits and let him take over. She bent forward a bit more, and it seemed like his dick began to hit a different spot and her pussy got a bit tighter.

She was rubbing herself against him for clitoral stimulation and her internal muscles kept gripping him. They came at the same time. This is the laziest Malcolm had ever had the pleasure of being during sex.

She pulled him out of her and held the condom in place. She reached over him again for some tissue and pulled the condom off of him and tossed it into the trash beside her bed. She lowered herself onto his chest. He pulled his arm from beneath her and wrapped it around her.

Placing his hand on her butt and squeezing it, "You are pretty into my ass huh?"

"Absolutely. Next time I am going to have to turn you around before we cum, so I can see that sexy ass while you work this dick."

Augusta chuckled, "What makes you think there will be a next time?" "A man can dream and have faith that he will be blessed with this at least a few times." He popped her on the ass after that.

They dozed off for a bit. They also woke up at the same time. Malcolm got up first to relieve himself in her ensuite. A dramatic change from the guys' bathroom.

This bathroom had a floral scent, and everything was gold and purple. There was even a zebra print bath rug, but instead of white; it was purple in the print. She also had positive affirmations printed on the mirror.

"She believed she could, so she did." He washed his hands and came out. Augusta swung her legs out of bed. She said, "Can you grab us some water and snacks from the fridge? I am going to take a quick shower." She walked past him and into the bathroom.

She had a feather-like touch on his genitals while passing him. Malcolm figured that he could not really protest such a simple request, but he was really hoping not to run into her brothers.

Malcolm walked out into the kitchen stark naked. He did not see any quick snacks in the fridge, so he checked a couple of cabinets and then the pantry. He decided to make them sandwiches because he was really hungry and needed some energy to do Augusta again.

He really wanted to bend her over, so he could give her ass some proper attention. As he began to assemble things for the sandwiches, the front door opened and the twins walked in. Malcolm spun around, and they saw him with his dick hanging out, making a sandwich in their kitchen.

UNEXPECTED

They said at the same time, "Malcolm". They looked at each other. "How do you?" Then they said at the same time again, "Hooked up yesterday". Then for another time they said at the same time, "Yesterday". Malcolm could swear that he stopped breathing during this exchange.

They seemed to communicate with each other wordlessly. Brandon nodded at Allen. They approached him. Malcolm actually got a little scared. Allen took the bread that he forgot he was holding and put it down on the counter top.

Brandon grabbed his other hand and pulled him toward the living room. Allen touched his waist as he followed behind them. Malcolm stammered out, "Hey guys, there might be some misunderstanding." Brandon said, "You fucked us yesterday and today you fucked our sister, or you are just here waiting for us and making us food."

They seemed to be done talking, and they began to strip off their clothes. Malcolm wondered what the hell was happening. Why wasn't he running from this apartment?

Allen commanded, "Sit". Malcolm sat then Allen came to the side of him and got up on his knees on the couch. He had his dick in his hand and said to Malcolm, "Suck" ,and Malcolm followed instructions.

Brandon then put his mouth on Malcolm's penis and began to suck timidly at first. After a couple of licks, he said, "Ugh, tastes like rubber." Malcolm could not respond because Allen definitely had his fingers digging into Malcolm's scalp and thrusting forward into his mouth.

Should someone have asked him what he wanted? Probably not. He never said no, and he is sitting here very eager putting a lot of energy into giving Allen an amazing blow job and enjoying the one being given to him by Brandon.

Minutes go by, and Augusta makes a chuckling noise. "You all could have let me enjoy my toy alone for a day." Malcolm could not speak. Allen was still thrusting into his mouth. "Technically he was our toy first, we just didn't know that we shared yesterday."

Augusta said, "How is this shit happening again?" Allen and Brandon laughed and then Brandon seemed to be making shallower and quicker thrusts into his mouth. He could not see where Augusta went, but it sounded like she went into the kitchen to finish making a sandwich.

She then went back into her room. Brandon stopped sucking Malcolm's dick. He stood up and said, "I want in his ass. He fucked me really good yesterday." Allen pulled out of Malcolm's mouth, "Lucky you. He got a blow job from me then I needed to get to work."

Allen got off the couch and stood to the side of Malcolm on the floor. "You need help up man?" said Brandon. Was Malcolm going to agree to whatever they had planned? He put his hands on his knees and then stood up.

They began to walk towards their rooms. Brandon was about to open his door when Allen said, "We are not about to get in that little ass bed of yours." They went into Allen's room. It was just as messy as yesterday when Malcolm opened the door.

One of the twins slapped him on the ass and told him to get onto the bed. Now Malcolm was up on his knees on the bed and then Brandon said, "You know what to do. Hands and knees Mr. Will Penetrate You." One of the twins smacked his ass while the other reached around him and fondled his balls and dick.

Brandon slid onto the bed in front of him, naked. He rested part of his upper body on the headboard and spread his legs in front of Malcolm.

Once Brandon adjusted himself a little more into a comfortable position, he cupped the back of Malcolm's head and pulled it toward his dick. Malcolm opened wide and proceeded to constantly move up and down Brandon's length.

Allen was behind Malcolm during this time. It sounded like he was grabbing things or maybe even straightening up to Malcolm. Music came on, and it was dubstep music that Malcolm would have no idea what artist made it or even sampled from. Brandon tossed a bottle of lube and condoms onto the bed.

"So you were just going to fuck the whole family Malcolm?" Allen said this as he hit Malcolm with his hand on the ass. He then kept a steady rhythm of popping on Malcolm's thighs and both butt cheeks. "Did you think you were not going to get caught, or were you hoping for something like this?"

Malcolm did not attempt to pull his mouth away from Brandon's dick, he kept sucking on it like he was trying to get to the center of a Tootsie Roll pop. Allen finally popped him-- kind of hard on the ass and said, "Answer me, Malcolm, if you want some dick in this ass."

Brandon pulled his dick away, and you could see the trail of slob coming from Malcolm's mouth to Brandon's dick. Malcolm said, "Yes, yes I wanted this. Now fuck me!" The last part he said as he was dry humping in the air.

By this point, Malcolm was really worked up and excited. Malcolm leaned forward to try and capture Brandon's penis in his mouth. Brandon pulled his dick away and said, "Get the balls. Make sure you get under them too."

Malcolm proceeded to suck on Brandon's balls. Then he used his hand to lift them a little, and he tongued Brandon's ass hole and sucked and licked on Brandon's perineum. Brandon said, "Keep doing that, and you are going to get a load in the face before I have a chance to fuck that ass too."

This made Malcolm focus on the perineum even more. Malcolm then felt Allen tap his backside with his dick a few times then he felt Allen putting lubricant in his ass.

He fingered him a few times then he heard the condom wrapper rip apart. He felt Allen's penis nudging into his ass. Brandon pulled his dick away. Lucky for him because Malcolm bit down.

Allen started to rub his back soothingly and said, "Relax, relax, there you go, push back, relax". Allen kept nudging in slowly, but he did not back out. Brandon took this opportunity to slap Malcolm with his penis quite a few times.

When Malcolm thought he was ready to resume sucking, he opened his mouth and let his tongue out a little. Brandon said, "Keep your mouth open". He then proceeded to pop his dick on Brandon's tongue and occasionally thrust his dick into Malcolm's mouth. It drove Malcolm crazy with need; he barely noticed that Allen had stopped moving behind him.

Brandon pulled his dick away again and was lazily stroking it and tugging on his balls. Allen started doing rapid short thrusts, and Malcolm got lost into that. He felt incredible. Allen reached around him, put his hand on his chest, and they were both up on their knees on the bed. Allen never stopped thrusting into Malcolm.

Brandon turned and got on his knees facing Malcolm. He stroked Malcolm slowly, and Malcolm began to make unintelligible sounds in between saying *yes* repeatedly. He was overwhelmed with how good he felt being fucked and fondled.

Malcolm said, "Fuuuuccckkkk, I am about to come" as Brandon was now sucking on his dick. Brandon peeled away from him, snatched up one of the condoms, opened it and slid it down on Malcolm so that he would not come on the bed.

He played with Malcolm's balls and nodded at Allen. Allen released a loud shout and started thrusting even faster into Malcolm, and they both came. Allen pulled out of Malcolm and helped him to lay down on his back.

He didn't remove Malcolm's condom like he removed his, and he went out of his room and into the bathroom. Malcolm could slightly hear the running water over the music. Brandon had a phone in his hand when Malcolm looked over to him.

Brandon was changing the music to soft rock. He put the phone down on the dresser and got on the bed. He touched Malcolm's anus softly, ready for some more. Malcolm was tired, but his dick did stir for the potential excitement. Brandon chuckled, reached for the lube and reapplied some to Malcolm again. He put a condom on himself and was not as gentle as he went into Malcolm.

Malcolm bared down on him and Brandon leaned forward, bringing his chest to Malcolm's and began to kiss him. Brandon kept up a steady beat of thrusting in and out of Malcolm. Allen sat on the bed and watched them for a bit.

Allen sat up but kept thrusting into Malcolm. Allen reached over and fondled Malcolm's balls and penis. He said, "You like playing with us, don't you?"

"Yes, yes please." The *please* came out as a request. "You want my dick in your mouth, don't you?" Malcolm did not answer.

"I want it too bad to make you beg for it." Allen pinched Malcolm's nipple as he got up on his knees and then straddled Malcolm's face.

He lifted up his balls and put his anus and perineum over Malcolm's mouth. Malcolm sucked and licked at both enthusiastically. Allen backed up a bit then he put the tip of his dick in Malcolm's mouth.

Allen grabbed the headboard and really started to fuck Malcolm's face in quick strokes. Occasionally making Malcolm deep throat and in other strokes make Malcolm chase him to keep his dick in his mouth.

Brandon had slowed down in his thrusting, trying to keep himself from cuming too fast. He then began to tug on Malcolm's balls. All the sensation was overwhelming to Malcolm, and he began to cum again.

He forced himself to keep his mouth from closing as Allen began to cum into his mouth shooting cum into the back of his throat. Brandon pulled out of him, took the condom off, crawled up to Malcolm's face and proceeded to cum on Malcolm too.

Malcolm was exhausted. The twins headed to the bathroom and both returned with a warm washcloth. One cleaned off his penis after removing the soiled condom and then another gently wiped his face.

He was happy not to lift a limb. The twins worked together to pull the comforter over Malcolm, and they crawled in on either side of him. One of them turned off the light, and they cuddled Malcolm.

Malcolm woke up and realized that it had to be pretty late in the day because of how the sun was shining relatively high in the sky. He realized that he was not at home and lying in the bed between

Brandon and Allen. His clothes were not even in the same room.

Malcolm contemplated how he could get out of bed without waking the twins. His friends were not going to believe the night he had. He heard some movement in the hallway or kitchen and remembered how he also slept with Augusta last night and that his clothes were in her room.

Malcolm drew his knees up to his chest and used the headboard to stand straight up. He walked towards the foot of the bed and Brandon said, "Have a good night Malcolm" as he stepped off the bed.

Being startled caused him to lose some of his footing, but he caught himself before he hit the ground. He closed the door on his way out of the bedroom because he could not figure out what to say. Walking into the kitchen naked, he saw Augusta.

"What-- no goodbye kiss for me, Malcolm?" He was confused, he really did not know what to say, so he attempted humor. "I can give you one now in exchange for my clothes?"

She said, "Have you even washed your mouth out?" Malcolm considered asking if she was mad but decided not to. It was not like he knew how to fix it and apologizing seemed weird. "No, I guess I should head on home to fix that."

"I guess you need your clothes first."

He was already looking at her, but he finally took in her lite terry cloth robe. He wondered if she even had any panties on. He could see her nipples poking through the thin, pale pink material. His semi-erect penis got harder.

He felt a little bolder, "What do I need to do to retrieve my clothes, Augusta?" "My permission."

REPEAT

Augusta moved over to the counter and hopped up on it. She said, "Open the fridge and get the whipped cream. We will not discard you without breakfast. We are not savages."

Malcolm was surprised at how obedient he had been the past twenty hours or so, but this family was over delivering. He turned his back to Augusta and looked around the refrigerator for the whipped cream.

He found it on the bottom shelf, grabbed it, and turned it back around to find her with her robe open. He was delighted to see that she had on no undergarments. She said, "Eat up" and reclined fully onto the countertop while opening her legs wide.

Malcolm put whipped cream on her nipples and on top of her clit. He licked her nipples and then began to suck on them a bit harder. Augusta made an audible noise. After Malcolm sucked off all the whipped cream from her breast, he alternated between licking each nipple and pinching them. Augusta moaned again but louder. As her body grew kind of tense she said, "I need you to eat my pussy right now, Malcolm."

He moved down her body and put his face immediately between her legs. He licked her from her anus to her clit and then sucked on her clit. Augusta thrust up into his mouth. She was really enjoying how eager he was to please.

He licked her seam and then proceeded to finger her while sucking on her clit again. Augusta came on his tongue hard but by this time Malcolm's dick was rock hard. He pulled away from her; she sat up a little and said, "I guess I can take care of that."

Malcolm picked her up and then turned her. Her pussy was in his face, and his dick was popped into her mouth. She wrapped her legs around his shoulders and neck loosely. They proceeded to give each other blow jobs as he walked them back to her room.

Once they were in Augusta's room, Malcolm deposited her onto her bed. She nodded to the bedside table where the rest of the condoms remained. He also saw his clothes neatly folded on his dresser.

His dick was extremely hard, and he could see her slickness. He didn't give a fuck about those clothes or meeting his friends on time. He put a condom on, tossed the wrapper onto the floor and thrust immediately into Augusta.

"Yes, Malcolm, fucking yes!" She repeated that as she wrapped her legs around him. Her ankles resting just below his lower back, occasionally digging into him as she lifted her hips to meet him for his thrusts.

Malcolm leaned back, causing her to drop her ankles. He put one hand around her throat and applied pressure to the sides, ensuring that he did not press on her windpipe and proceeded to give her longer, slower strokes. Being choked got her so excited that she came quickly after, but he had a few more in him.

Malcolm pulled out, flipped her over, and popped her on the butt. He put his hands on her waist and yanked her back--jerking her to her hands and knees and drove back into her. He thrust into her fast and hard.

He was not being gentle with her at all. He took one hand from her waist and put it into her hair. He pulled it back as he continued to fuck her harder.

Malcolm felt the strong urge to cum, so he pulled out of Augusta, took the rubber off and came on her butt. Augusta chuckled and said, "Well you could have at least put that protein in my mouth."

Malcolm was amazed. She took that like a champ. He was rougher with her than he had been with any other woman. Malcolm laughed and began to put on his clothes. He saw the time on her clock and knew he was going to get an ear full from his friends. Malcolm really needed a shower.

BRUNCH REALIZATIONS

Jacob said, "I do not think you are the king. I think your story makes you the servant. You got passed around like a hot potato." Frank retorted, "Maybe more like a puppy. He looks happy that everyone played with him. No one wants the potato."

Tracie said, "He could also just be the dirty bath water." Grace said, "You are definitely not king. You just had a little fun." Jacob added, "He had more than a little fun."

Tracie pondered out loud, "Malcolm, do you think the three of them have done someone together before?" Malcolm replied, "Shit if they have, I feel cheated." The table erupted in laughter.

Grace said, "Now allow me to trample all over Malcolm's supposedly interesting story. You all will not believe what I went through to get my stuff from TSA and into my apartment. It was all ridiculous, but some of the dick was marvelous."

ACKNOWLEDGEMENT

Thank you to Chelsea Green for sitting next to me at that reception and asking me what I have been up to. In you I found an editor and you have been a saving grace for me to finish and submit my work.

Thank you to all my friends who would ask me every month when I would release my work because they were ready to support.

Thank you very much for reading! I hope you become a subscriber at mcbyrdauthor.com

ABOUT THE AUTHOR

M.c. Byrd

M.C. has been a lover of books since she was a child and her grandmother bought her a set of 100 boks that everyone should read. She mostly read her grandmas steamy novels instead.

You can find her typing away in Texas or next to you on a plane or train enjoying her next adventure.

DEBAUCHED SQUAD GOALS

Take a journey at brunch with Malcolm, Grace, Frank, Tracie and Jacob. Hear about their sexual experiences that stretch kinks and interests.

Sleeping With Neighbors

Resolving Flight Changes

My Admin Takes Control